Who's a Big Bully Then?

by

Michael Morpurgo

Illustrated by Joanna Carey

You do not need to read this page –
just get on with the book!

Published in 2000 in Great Britain by
Barrington Stoke Ltd, Sandeman House, Trunk's Close,
55 High Street, Edinburgh EH1 1SR
www.barringtonstoke.co.uk

Reprinted 2001, 2002 (twice), 2003, 2004, 2005

ISBN 1-902260-43-0

Printed in Great Britain by Bell & Bain Ltd

MEET THE AUTHOR - MICHAEL MORPURGO

What is your favourite animal?
Elephant
What is your favourite boy's name?
George
What is your favourite girl's name?
Eleanor
What is your favourite food?
Prawns
What is your favourite music?
'Spem in Alium' by Thomas Tallis
What is your favourite hobby?
Writing

MEET THE ILLUSTRATOR - JOANNA CAREY

What is your favourite animal?
My cat, Alfie
What is your favourite boy's name?
I have three favourites - Joseph, Felix and Daniel
What is your favourite girl's name?
Amy
What is your favourite food?
Smoked salmon
What is your favourite music?
Bach piano music
What is your favourite hobby?
Making things out of things

For Joanna who helped make
this book

Contents

Chapter 1
Darren Bishop

It all began with Darren Bishop. Any trouble I have at school always begins with Darren Bishop. He's been on my back all year, ever since I first came to this school. Darren Bishop is big, very big. He is big everywhere – big neck, big arms, big head. He has the biggest head in the whole school, in the whole world probably, and I hate him. I hate him like poison.

I'm also frightened of him, so I do my very best to keep out of his way whenever I can. But sooner or later, almost everyday, I bump into him.

Some days I've even bunked off school just to avoid him. I'm that scared of him. I don't know why he picks on me. Maybe it's because I'm a bit small and skinny. All I know is that he does everything he can to make my life a misery.

He's called me every nasty name he can think of. 'Chicken', 'little git' and 'baby face' are his favourites. When he really wants to wind me up he calls me 'a lily-livered, stinking coward'. I think he got that off some film on the television.

And it's not just name-calling either. He's always making horrible faces at me or flicking out my tie or giving me a shove.

But I keep my cool, even when he kicks my bag and stamps all over my books. He's done that twice now.

I don't keep my cool because I'm brave. It's just that I know he wants me to have a go at him, to start something, so that he'll have an excuse to beat me up. And he would too. But I'm not stupid. Nothing he did was ever going to make me fight him. Not his way anyway.

Then last week I had a chance, a lucky chance, to get my own back.

My way, on my terms.

Chapter 2
Sports Day

It was Sports Day. I've never been much good at ball games, like football or basketball or volleyball. I just get pushed around all the time. But running, that's a different thing altogether. I can "go like a whippet", that's what my father says. So I was really looking forward to Sports Day.

My best distance is 200 metres. I'd got through my heats easily enough and there I was lined up in the sun for the final. There were eight of us all ready and waiting for the gun. And right beside me, in the next lane, was big Darren Bishop. This was my chance and I was going to take it.

My father had come to watch. He hardly ever comes into school. He's always too busy on the farm, but he always comes to see me run on Sports Day. And I know why too. He loves to see me win.

He was pretty fast himself when he was a kid. That's what he tells me anyway. That's where I get it from, he says. In the genes, he says, whatever they are. There he was in the crowd already getting himself all excited. (Mum won't come because he leaps up and down and shouts his head off and it embarrasses her.)

"Go on, son," he was shouting. "You can do it. Don't look around, son. Run low out of the blocks. Get those legs pumping."

I waved at him, more to shut him up than anything else. It wasn't that I didn't want him there. I did. But he shouts so loudly that people notice him and laugh at him and I hate that.

Darren Bishop had noticed him and was laughing at him.

"What a nerd! Your Dad, he looks a right nerd." And he said it loud enough for everyone to hear. "Is he drunk or something?"

I was really riled up, but I made myself look the other way and say nothing. Darren hadn't finished with me yet.

"What's it like to have a little git for a Dad?" he went on. "Two little gits in the same family. Three maybe. Your Mum's a little git too, isn't she?"

That was it. I'd had enough. I turned on him like an angry terrier. If it was a fight he wanted, then he could have one, right now. It was only the starter who saved me.

"Are you ready? To your marks. Get set."

Bang! We were off. I was really fired up, but not to win. I didn't care about winning the race any more. All I wanted to do was beat big Darren Bishop. I just wanted to whip him in front of everyone.

He went storming off. He was already miles ahead and going like a train. But I knew he'd gone off too fast. I hung back and just let him think he was winning, let him puff himself right out.

The crowd was going wild, because they could see what Darren couldn't see. I was coming up through the field, going faster

and faster all the time, until there was only Darren left to overtake.

Then I was right alongside him, and big Darren Bishop was beginning to slow, beginning to tire. He glanced across at me and I could see in his eyes that he knew he was beaten.

"You don't look so good," I said. "You feeling all right? Long way to go yet, long way for a big lump like you." And I just cruised past him and away from him, waving as I went.

"I'll get you, little git," he shouted after me. "I'll get you."

"Byee," I shouted over my shoulder. "Byee."

I was really enjoying myself. I had never in all my life run as fast as I was running now. My legs just seemed to flow over the ground. I was coming into the straight. I had a quick look behind me. Darren Bishop looked as if he was going backwards! I went streaking towards the tape and on either side of me the crowd was leaping up and down.

And there was my father yelling his head off and running out onto the track to wave me on. I raised my hands in the air and felt the tape wrap around my chest. I had won. It was the best moment of my life.

I looked around. There he was, big Darren Bishop, lumbering down the straight puffing and blowing, his face bright red. I had whipped him in front of the whole school and it felt great.

Everyone crowded round me. Mr Griffiths, 'Whiffy Griffy', the headteacher, came up to me and shook my hand.

"Great stuff," he said. "Go on like that, and you'll be in the Olympics one day."

My father was standing there glowing with pride. Everyone was clapping me on the back and congratulating me – well, not quite everyone. I never saw Darren Bishop after the race. He just disappeared. Out of sight, out of mind, they say.

****

It wasn't true though, not that day, not for me. I was loving it all, all the congratulations, all the fuss, and the gold medal Whiffy Griffy presented me with. But over all of it hung Darren's horrible threat.

"I'll get you," he'd said. "I'll get you."

I couldn't get his words out of my head. I didn't know when, I didn't know where, but I knew that sooner or later he'd be coming after me.

As it turned out, it was sooner rather than later.

Chapter 3
The Plan

It was in morning break the following Monday. Suddenly I saw him coming towards me across the playground, and he was bringing his whole horrible crowd with him. I looked around. There was nowhere to run to. I was cornered, like a rat in a trap.

I tried to make out I wasn't scared. But I was. I was scared rigid. I felt a warm tingle

of fear creeping up the back of my neck. This was it. I was for it now, really for it.

"Your time's up, baby face," Darren said, shoving me against the wall and pushing his face into mine. "I've come to get you, just like I said I would. You know what you are? You're chicken. You're a coward, a lily-livered, yellow coward. Aren't you?" And he pushed me again.

"No, I'm not," I said, sounding as tough as I could.

"Fight!" someone shouted. "Fight!"

By now the whole school seemed to be crowding round.

"All right, all right," I went on, "if it's a fight you're looking for ...." I was playing for time, trying to think of a way out, any way out.

Darren grabbed me by the tie and jerked me towards him.

"I'm going to mash you to pulp, yellow pulp, and I'm going to enjoy every moment of it. I'm a bully, a big bully. I'm the biggest bully in the school and I like it. Do you know why? Because I get to beat up namby-pamby little gits like you."

That's the funny thing. It was Darren himself bragging about being a bully that gave me my idea, my utterly brilliant idea.

"All right, I'll fight you," I said, "but not like this, not here. What's the point? No fun for anyone, is it? I mean, everyone knows you'd win, don't they?"

Darren Bishop didn't quite know what to make of this. I'd taken the wind right out of his sails. While he was thinking about it

(Darren Bishop thinks *very slowly*), I went on, "You called me a coward, right?"

"No," said Darren, "I called you a lily-livered, yellow coward." And he thumped me hard in the chest, knocking the breath right out of me.

"What about you?" I said, when I could speak again. "Who's to say you're not a coward as well? I mean, we're all frightened of something. Everyone is."

"Well, I'm not," Darren replied. "I'm not frightened of anything."

"You sure of that, are you?" I asked.

"Yeah, baby face, quite sure. Just you try me."

Brilliant. Just as I thought he would, he'd fallen right into my trap.

"All right," I said. "You know Mr Langdon's farm, where those big sheds are just outside town, beyond the football ground on the left hand side? You know the place? I'll meet you there. Six o'clock tomorrow morning. There'll be no one about."

"What for?" Darren asked. I could tell he was getting worried.

"A sort of challenge. A sort of dare. A sort of duel, to find out who the coward is, you or me."

"What if it's all a trick?" Darren definitely didn't like it. He was trying to get out of it. I could feel him wriggling and I wasn't going to let him off the hook. "What if you just don't turn up?" he said.

"Oh, I'll be there," I told him. "And if I'm not, then you can mash me into pulp some other time, can't you? All right?"

Chapter 4
Dawn

So it was all arranged. We'd all meet at
Mr Langdon's farm at dawn the next day.
Just the right time for a duel.

The thing is, I live quite close to Mr
Langdon's farm. Only just down the road in
fact. It's where my father works. He's
always worked there. He does all sorts. He
sees to the sheep, all the shearing and the
lambing. He feeds the pigs, he makes the
hay, harvests the corn and he looks after

nearly fifty beef cows, Ruby Reds, the most beautiful cows in the world.

I almost grew up on the farm and just like my father, I love the cows best of all. All right, so they leave little messy messages here and there. So what? And where there's cows you have to have a bull. It's only natural.

We've got this bull, a massive, humungously huge, reddy brown bull with horns that are long and curved and pointed, just like Vikings have on the sides of their helmets. He's called Olympus or 'Olly' for short. Olly's a bit old now. He's nice and quiet – he always has been. I've known him just about all my life. My father used to sit me on his back when I was little – he's that quiet, honestly.

Of course, Darren Bishop was a town boy like almost everyone in my school. He did

not know one bull from another, if you see what I mean. I mean he thought what most people think, that bulls charge you, all bulls, particularly if you're wearing red. He had no idea that Olly, though he looked humungously nasty, was in fact as gentle as a lamb.

I knew he'd be scared silly. Just the thought of it was already making me chuckle, making me chuckle a lot. It was perfect. The whole set-up, the whole plan was perfect.

The next morning dawned misty and cold. I crept out of the house and ran down the lane. They were already waiting, perhaps twenty of them in all, their bikes leaning up against the farm shed. Darren was there and his breath was sending smoke signals in the air as he came towards me.

"Well, baby face," he scoffed, "what's this so-called challenge of yours, then?"

"You'll see," I replied coolly. "It's this way, not far."

I climbed over the fence into the field, and they came after me. We walked and walked, and as we walked the mist became thicker and thicker. All the time they asked me where we were going and I said nothing except, "You'll see."

At the gate into the meadow I stopped and waited until they were all there. Then I spoke in a hushed voice. "He's in here," I said.

"Who is?" Darren asked. "And what are you whispering for anyway?"

I put my finger to my lips. "Sssh!" I whispered. "He doesn't like a lot of noise.

It makes him angry. And we don't want him angry, do we?"

"Who?" Darren shouted. He was really riled up now.

"The bull," I whispered, but loud enough for all of them to hear. I went on, "Listen, there's a big bull in this field with horns, *big* horns. He's out there somewhere in all that mist. I'm going to find him and I'm going to catch him. I'm going to lead him round the field by the horn. Then you're going to do the same. All right? That's the challenge, that's the dare. You're not frightened, are you?"

There was a very long silence before Darren spoke up. "Course not," he said. He was whispering now.

But when I opened the gate to go into
the field, none of them seemed to want to
come with me.

"Come on," I said. "You won't be able to
see anything if you don't come in."

They came just inside the gate, but no
further. So I went alone out into the
mist-covered field.

"Where are you?" I called out. "Where are you? Who's a big bully then? Who's a big bully?"

I didn't have too long to wait. I could hear his hooves thundering. I could feel the earth shaking.

And then he came charging out of the mist towards me, tossing his head and snorting. It was brilliant, better than I could have hoped for. He looked every bit like a raging, fighting bull. But I knew my Olly. He soon slowed to a walk. Then he stopped and looked at me out of his wild, wide eyes.

"Who's a big bully then?" I said, loudly now, so they could all hear how brave I was.

Olly began pawing the ground, lowering his head at me and tossing his horns playfully. *I* knew it was playfully, but they

didn't. I turned round to wave at Darren and the others. For some reason he was already on the other side of the gate. They all were.

"It's all right," I called out. "He's a nice bully. Watch this."

Then I walked right up to Olly and
patted his neck. Then I scratched him
between his horns where I knew he liked it.
He stood quite still, snorting at me like he
always did when he was pleased to see me.
His breath smelt milky on the air. A dozen
of his lady friends came wandering out of
the mist, mooing for him. Olly lifted his

head and roared back, a terrifying bellow that echoed all around the valley.

I waited till the echoes had died away.

"Listen, Olly," I whispered. "You see those boys by the gate. They think you're a fighting sort of bull, a real killer and that's what I want them to go on thinking. So don't look soft, all right? Look vicious, Olly.

Can you do that for me? I want you to scare
them silly."

And Olly tossed his head again and
swished his tail. Then I had the coolest idea
I'd ever had. I took off my coat and began to
flap it at him, like a matador's cape.

"Olé, Olly!" I cried. "Olé!"

Olly snorted at me angrily. He lifted his
head and showed me the whites of his eyes.
I'd never seen him look so vicious. He was
playing his part perfectly. Then I knelt
down in front of him just like matadors do
and shook my coat at him. Olly pawed the
ground, kicking up great clods of earth.

"Well done, Olly," I whispered. "That's
brilliant, just brilliant. Now I'm going to
walk you over to meet them. Look nasty,
right? And I mean *mean*, really mean."

I got up, took Olly by the horn and led him slowly towards the gate. Big Darren Bishop and the others were already backing away, gaping at us as we came. Darren had gone white around the lips.

"Your turn," I said sweetly, opening the gate. "Come on in. Easy as falling off a log. Honest."

Darren ran. They all ran. They bolted like frightened rabbits, scattering into the mist and leaving me alone with Olly.

How I laughed! I laughed till I cried. When I'd done laughing – and that took some time – I put my arms around Olly's neck and thanked him.

"You're the best bull in the world, Olly," I said. "Who's a big bully boy! Olé, Olly! Olé!" And I laughed all over again.

Chapter 5
Who's a Big Bully Then?

I ran all the way home. I couldn't wait to tell my parents all about it, about how I had tricked big Darren Bishop. They were already having breakfast and they didn't look at all pleased with me.

"Where the devil have you been?" my father asked. "We've been looking everywhere."

"I've been worried sick," said my mother. "How many times do I have to tell you not to go off like that without telling us?"

"Well?" my father went on. "What have you been up to then?"

"Let him have his breakfast first," my mother said. "Or else he'll be late for school."

So as I ate my breakfast, I told them the whole story from beginning to end. After a bit I noticed my father was looking at me strangely and my mother had gone quite pale. They kept looking at each other as I told them about what I'd been up to with Olly.

"I knelt down right in front of him and I did all that matador stuff, y'know, flapping my coat at him. He was great. You should

46

have seen him, Dad. He was pawing the ground and ..."

"You did *what*?" my father shouted. "You did *what*?"

"I was just playing, Dad. Then I just took him by the horn and walked him across the field. You should've seen me, Mum. Olly was great. Gentle as a lamb. Darren and his lot, they all thought he was like a fighting bull, a real killer bull."

My mother had her head in her hands.

"What's wrong?" I asked. "What's the matter?"

"What's wrong? What's wrong?" My father's voice was squeaking. He was upset, really upset. "I'll tell you what's wrong. That bull you knelt down in front of, that bull you led around the field, that bull wasn't Olly. I brought Olly inside the shed a couple of days ago now. He's got a bad foot. So we had to borrow Mr Weldon's bull to take his place with the cows. And Mr Weldon's bull, Samson they call him, is just about the meanest, nastiest, most vicious bull I have ever come across. That's what's wrong."

I didn't want to eat my cornflakes after that. They'd gone all soggy. I just wanted to be sick, but when I got up to go to the toilet I found my knees were soggy too.

I didn't want to go to school at all. I said I felt too sick – but they made me. By the time I got there, the story was all round the school – how I had knelt down in front of a raging wild bull and how big Darren Bishop had chickened out. I was the hero of the hour, top of the pops, King of the Castle.

And Darren Bishop hadn't even dared show his face. He'd stayed off school.

It should have been the happiest day of my life, but it wasn't. I felt far too sick to enjoy a single moment of it.

A Letter from the Author

Dear Reader,

Do you want to know something? That happened, that really happened to me? Not the bullying part of the story you've just read, but the farm bit at the end ...

Many years ago now, I went into a field on the farm where I live in Devon, walked right up to the bull and patted him – because I knew he was gentle. (I still felt very brave.)

That evening the farmer said to me when I met him in the lane, "Best be careful, Michael, if you go into the field where the bull is. He's a new one, only been here since yesterday. And he can be a bit mean, a bit wicked."

To me the bulls had looked exactly the same!

I didn't feel brave any longer. Funny how you can be frightened after the event is all over.

****

Maybe I should tell you a little about the farm where I live, because it's not an ordinary farm at all.

Most farms have cows or sheep or pigs or hens or geese or ducks. So does our farm. But our farm has children too, a thousand of them every year. (Not all at once!) They don't come just for a trailer ride and a walk round, they come for a whole week to help run the farm. They become the farm workers! And I mean *workers*. Just so long as it's safe, the children do it. (They don't go into the field with the bull, for instance!)

And it's a *real* farm, not a play farm where you come to cuddle a lamb and stroke a horse, though they do that too.

It's a huge farm too. It's about as big as 250 football pitches. There are 80 milking cows, 500 sheep, 40 pigs, 100 beef cattle, 50 calves, 35 ducks, 42 hens, 3 geese, 3 donkeys, a horse and all the farm cats and dogs you could wish for.

The teachers and children who come all live together in a huge Victorian manor house which becomes their home for a week.

There are dormitories for the children, a playroom (we call it the 'noisy room') with ping-pong and table football, a classroom and a 'quiet room', a sort of sitting room and library all in one.

Outside there's a five-acre field to run in, as big as Wembley, with cowpats for goal posts. Nice and squidgy!

Here's what the children do in the mornings with their teachers and the farmers who work on the farm with us.

7 am: Get up. Have a cup of tea. Out on the farm in three working groups (12 in each). One group goes to milk the cows. Another goes to feed the pigs and calves. Another feeds the horse and donkeys, and opens up the hens and ducks and geese. Back for breakfast.

9.30 am: Out onto the farm again, one group brushing down the dairy, another feeding or moving sheep, another putting the horse and donkeys out, another cleaning out the stables, feeding the hens and ducks and geese.

11 am: Have a bit of a break and a drink and a biscuit too. (We need it!)

After breaktime, sometimes it's work in the classroom, sometimes it's playtime.

After lunch, we go out onto the farm in our three groups to work again on farm

tasks which means anything that needs to be done, depending on what time of year it is, and on the weather.

So we clean out sheds (lots of these). Bring in logs for the fires, pick up apples and potatoes (at harvest time), pick raspberries, strawberries (there's a huge, walled vegetable garden where we grow our own vegetables) and blackberries from the hedgerows. We help with the corn and harvesting by stacking up the bales for the loader. There is always something to do, I promise you, and something useful too.

We have three good, hot meals a day. (I don't do the cooking, which is lucky for the children!) Supper is at five and then at six o'clock off we go again.

But now the groups change (so that everyone does all the farm jobs at least four times a week). There's the milking to be done, the pigs and calves to be fed, the horse and donkeys to be brought in and groomed, the eggs to be collected, the hens and ducks and geese to be shut up, in case the fox comes. And he does come all too often.

We come back to the house by about 7.30 pm (it's called Nethercott House) for a hot chocolate and a story. I go up once a week to read them a story. And one of my favourites is *Who's a Big Bully Then?*

If you or your teacher or your Mum or Dad would like to know more about the farm visits – we call it Farms for City Children, then you can write to me, Michael Morpurgo, at:

Nethercott House
Iddesleigh
Winkleigh
Devon
EX9 8BG

Farms for City Children is a charity
with three such farms – one in Wales, one
in Gloucestershire and one here in Devon.
We now welcome over three thousand
primary school children from our towns
and cities every year.

Maybe your school would like to come
too. I hope so.

All the best,

Michael Morpurgo

Who is Barrington Stoke?

Barrington Stoke was a famous and much-loved story-teller. He travelled from village to village carrying a lantern to light his way. He arrived as it grew dark and when the young boys and girls of the village saw the glow of his lantern, they hurried to the central meeting place. They were full of excitement and expectation, for his stories were always wonderful.

Then Barrington Stoke set down his lantern. In the flickering light the listeners were enthralled by his tales of adventure, horror and mystery. He knew exactly what they liked best and he loved telling a good story. And another. And then another. When the lantern burned low and dawn was nearly breaking, he slipped away. He was gone by morning, only to appear the next day in some other village to tell the next story.

Barrington Stoke would like to thank all its readers for commenting on the manuscript before publication and in particular:

Steven Forsyth
Lawrence Gripper
Laurie Hunter-Pratt
Heather Moore
Jenna Neill
Craig Smail
Alison Waugh

Become a Consultant!

Would you like to give us feedback on our titles before they are published? Contact us at the email address or website below – we'd love to hear from you!

E-mail: info@barringtonstoke.co.uk
Website: www.barringtonstoke.co.uk

Barrington Stoke would like to thank all its readers for commenting on the manuscript before publication and in particular:

Steven Forsyth
Lawrence Gripper
Laurie Hunter-Pratt
Heather Moore
Jenna Neill
Craig Smail
Alison Waugh

Barrington Stoke Club

Would you like to become a member of our club? Children who write to us with their views become members of our club and special advisors to the company. They also have the chance to act as editors on future manuscripts. Contact us at the address or website below – we'd love to hear from you!

Barrington Stoke, 10 Belford Terrace, Edinburgh EH4 3DQ
Tel: 0131 315 4933 Fax: 0131 315 4934
E-mail: info@barringtonstoke.co.uk
Website: www.barringtonstoke.co.uk